'decorative and fertile . . . profuse and dainty drawings . . .'
Sunday Times

'delightful'
What's On in London

'guaranteed to keep the inquisitive young reader entertained . . .
Quirky humour and zany features add to the attraction for readers of all ages.'
Inis

'crowded with hilarious characters and interesting images . . . A delightful book.'
Booktrusted News

To a very brave little boy and his mum,
Oscar and Emmie O'Kane

Also by Sally Gardner
The Glass Heart · The Fairy Catalogue · A Book of Princesses
The Real Fairy Storybook (text by Georgie Adams)

The Strongest Girl in the World · The Smallest Girl Ever
The Boy Who Could Fly · The Invisible Boy · The Boy with the Magic Numbers

First published in Great Britain in 2003
by Orion Children's Books
This paperback edition first published in 2004
by Dolphin Paperbacks
a division of the Orion Publishing Group Ltd
Orion House
5 Upper Saint Martin's Lane
London WC2H 9EA

Text and illustrations copyright © Sally Gardner 2003

Design by Helen Ewing

The right of Sally Gardner to be identified as the author and illustrator of this work has been asserted.

A catalogue record for this book is available from the British Library

Printed and bound in Italy

Sally Gardner

Fairy Shopping

Dolphin

Welcome to the wonderful world of fairy shops! Anything you want can be yours by wishing.

so let me take you to Silverbell Street on a shopping spree.

Just remember – if you don't believe in fairies, you won't see anything at all!

A treat to start with!

SPARKLE DIPS SWEETSHOP

A twist of magic

Bags of sweet delights

SIMPLE SIMON

THE LITTLE RED HEN

SINGING PIES · CAKES THAT C
· REAL LIVE GINGER BREAD

HELP
NEEDED

The sweetshop sells lollipops that sing to you,
goblin gobstoppers, and witches' toffee
that turns your ears from red to blue.

Over there are the butchers,
the bakers and the
candlestick makers.

Here's the hat shop. A hat can change your life, find you a prince or make you a wife.

You can't go shopping in Silverbell Street without visiting Ali Baba's shop. It's a treasure trove!

I'm looking for a magic mirror, an old oil lamp,
three beans,
a broom,
a clock that strikes midnight only, and a tinderbox. . . .

Special Offer on Goldilocks!
Princesses for frogs!

DRAGON DREAMS

Stitch in Time

STYLISH
OUTFITS
FOR THE
FOX
ABOUT
TOWN

LOUNGE LIZARD

This is the pet shop
where pets choose their owners.

This shop here has embroidered waistcoats
stitched by mice.

There's a shop
with made-to-measure suits for wolves,
hunting jackets for foxes,
and dressing-gowns for dragons.

Oh good, it's time for elevenses.

This is the café where Mr Wolf has his breakfast every day.
Don't be put off by the bats' brew – they do some very tasty buns as well.

Now, let's see who's in here that you might know.

To market, to market to buy a fat pig! Lots of hustle and bustle and much more besides!

Fill your basket with whatever you wish, but beware of the goblins.
They'd sell you their grandmothers if they could.

I spy with my little eye . . .

SECOND-HAND CLOTHES FROM FIRST-RATE FAIRY TALES!

BEANSTALK FOR SALE

special deals and spinning wheels

What can you spy?

PAMPER YOUR FROG!

PIXIE PIE

Fairy Furnishings

Witch Face Remover

BLUEBEARD'S

Hats for Cats

This is where witches go
to get green hand cream
for blue nails.

You can get all the latest magic tricks
in Mr Farfunkel's magic shop.

Did you say you wanted a magic ring?
This shop has the sparkliest jewellery any fairy could wish for.

That reminds me, I need a new spell
to make me invisible.

And I need a flying umbrella
and a weather vane that makes the sun shine.

Let me take you to the Foxglove Restaurant, where the fairies come for lunch to meet their friends.

I thought you'd like to have a look round this shop.
Take your time. I need to have a word with Blossom about a ballgown.

If you want a whiff of real fairy magic, look no further. Here they sell perfumed oil lamps with genies in.
And if you need to drown out dragon pong, you can buy some Fairy Breeze.

I always buy my wands and wings from Sparks & Twinkle.

You wouldn't believe how many spells go wrong!

That's the greengrocer, and just along from there is Miss Prism's Gift Shop.
Oh look, three wishes in a beautiful gift-wrapped box!
What a lovely present for a friend who's down in the dumps!

Over there you can get clothes for giants, with boots in large sizes up to 10 gallons.

Shall we stop for some tea,
and some of those fairy cakes that fly?

This shop is run by a bad-tempered witch.
You can get ingredients for your cauldron
so you too can brew up trouble.

And this shop caters for the sheepish shopper,
with off-the-peg clothes for pigs and pussycats.

Thumbelina sells frocks
from the famous Tulip range,
all in teeny-weeny sizes. . .

and her friend Tom Thumb
sells charming clothes
for the little chaps . . .

and oh good!
there's the toyshop!

It's getting dark. Look, the fairy lights are coming on!
The shops are closing and it's time for me to be going home.

I'm sad to say goodbye. I hope you've enjoyed our shopping trip.
Did you get everything you wanted? Don't worry if you didn't, you can always come back.
I'll be here in Silverbell Street, waiting for you.